W9-ANY-483

Kongi and Potgi

A Cinderella Story from Korea

adapted by Oki S. Han
and Stephanie Haboush Plunkett
pictures by Oki S. Han

Dial Books for Young Readers New York

In memory of my mother
O.S.H.

In memory of my father, Joseph Haboush
S.H.P.

Published by Dial Books for Young Readers
A Division of Penguin Books USA Inc.
375 Hudson Street
New York, New York 10014

Typography by Amelia Lau Carling
Printed in Hong Kong

First Edition
1 3 5 7 9 10 8 6 4 2

Library of Congress Cataloging in Publication Data
Han, Oki S.
Kongi and Potgi: a Cinderella story from Korea/
adapted by Oki S. Han and Stephanie Haboush Plunkett;
pictures by Oki S. Han.—1st ed. p.   cm.
Summary: Although Kongi is treated unfairly by her stepmother
and stepsister, she proves she is worthy to become the prince's bride.
ISBN 0-8037-1571-4 (tr.).—ISBN 0-8037-1572-2 (lib.)
[1. Fairy tales. 2. Folklore—Korea.] I. Plunkett, Stephanie Haboush.
II. Cinderella. Korean. III. Title.
PZ8.H18288Ko 1996   398.21—dc20   [E]   93-28426   CIP   AC

The art for each picture consists of a watercolor painting,
which is scanner-separated and reproduced in full-color.

Some Facts About Korean Culture

"Kongi and Potgi" (pronounced Con-jee and Pot-jee) is one of Korea's most popular tales for children.

Korea is a mountainous country, but fertile farmlands can be found in the river valleys and along the coast. Before the 1900's Korea was an agricultural society. Almost all the people lived in small villages and worked on farms. Rice has always been the most important crop, and a main part of any Korean meal. In fact, the word for cooked rice, *pap*, has come to mean "food" or "meal."

Houses in rural Korea usually had two to four rooms, walls of wood, clay, or pounded earth, and a tile or thatch roof. Floors made of thick stone slabs or hard dirt were covered with oiled paper or mats. And warmth in the winter was provided by the *ondol*—passages under the floors that carried hot air from the stove or fireplace to each of the rooms.

Large ceramic pots that held soy sauce, bean paste, and hot red pepper sauce, often used in Korean cooking, stood outside the house in a sunny spot. On nice days their lids would be left open to allow the sauces to "breathe." One of the jars was always filled with water that had been drawn from the village well.

Outdoor marketplaces provided village residents with everything that they could need or want. Vendors from near and far sold fish, grains, vegetables, and clothing such as the traditional black hat *(got)* and straw shoes *(gyeep shin)*. Even donkeys, hens, cats, and other animals were available for purchase.

In Korean folktales, spirits in the form of animals, ogres, and goblins have the power to trouble or protect their earthly relatives as they choose. According to ancient beliefs, these spirits may be those of deceased ancestors. The appearance of the kind ox, frog, sparrows, and angels in *Kongi and Potgi* may represent attempts by Kongi's deceased mother to help her through difficult times.

Many years ago in a peaceful Korean village, there lived a kind-hearted girl named Kongi.

Kongi and her parents lived happily, until suddenly Kongi's mother became ill. The village doctors tried to cure her, but soon she died. Deeply saddened by her loss, Kongi was comforted by her loving father. After a time she overcame her great sorrow.

One evening Kongi's father spoke to her gently. "You are growing so quickly, and will need a woman's hand to guide you. There is a lady named Doki who seems generous and kind. Her own daughter is just your age, and what good friends you could be! I would like to ask her to be my wife."

Kongi knew that her father had been lonely and was glad he had found a companion. After the wedding Doki and her daughter Potgi moved into the house.

"Welcome," said Kongi politely. "I hope that you will be comfortable here."

"We certainly shall," smiled her stepmother, who stroked her hair sweetly.

But Potgi just glared at her coldly, which made her uneasy.

"What a fine family we'll be," said Kongi's father, and all seemed to agree.

The next day, though, everything changed. When Kongi's father left for work, her stepmother spoke to her harshly. "Stop dreaming," she said. "I'll certainly not be *your* servant!" She and Potgi made her do all their chores. And that night they scolded her even in front of her father. Shocked, he begged his wife to be more understanding. But when his pleas went unanswered, he said no more, hoping to keep peace in his household.

Poor Kongi! It seemed as though the pleasant times she once shared at home with her parents were gone forever. "My Potgi needs a soft bed to sleep on," said her stepmother, pushing Kongi into the cold room off the pantry. That night as Kongi listened to the field mice scurry across the floor, she longed to be back in her bedroom, surrounded by the lovely things that once belonged to her mother. Kongi missed her now more than ever.

As time passed, Kongi's once rosy cheeks turned pale and sallow. The backbreaking work exhausted her, but she never complained.

Each day when Kongi arrived at the spring, buried under heavy bundles of laundry, the village women were outraged. "She's wasting away!" they said. "Her stepmother makes her work far too hard."

"Oh, no," insisted Kongi. "She works at least as hard as I do," she said, blinking back her tears.

When the time came to clear the fields for planting, Doki called Kongi and Potgi together. "Potgi will work the field near the river, and Kongi will go to the land on the hillside," she said, handing each a hoe.

Potgi's work was finished quickly. The soil near the river was sandy, and her steel hoe easily plied the few stones from the ground.

But the land on the hillside was hard and rocky, and it seemed as though Kongi would never get done. "Oh, no!" she cried when her old wooden hoe finally broke. "What will I do now?"

"Mmmmoo," said an ox who appeared suddenly before her. "Don't worry, I will help you." He told her to rest, and gave her a juicy apple to eat. Astonished, Kongi watched as he pulled up weeds and heavy stones with his strong jaws, until the whole field had been cleared.

Meanwhile Potgi and her mother browsed leisurely in the marketplace, which was their favorite pastime. "Oh dear, it's getting late and Kongi's work is still not done," they sneered with obvious glee.

Just then they turned to see Kongi heading home with a big basket of apples. "You can't be finished already!" they cried.

"Well, I surely would not have been, were it not for a kind ox who stopped to help me. He even gave me these apples that I've brought to share with you."

"Don't be silly, Kongi. How can you tell such stories?" they said, amazed that her job was done.

As the weeks passed, the warmth of the sun brought the village to life. People prepared for a celebration, and when the May festival finally came, everyone was excited—especially Kongi. Her step-mother had other plans for her, however. "The water jar is as dry as a bone. Won't you fill it before you go?" she said.

Kongi set out to fill the jar with water for washing and cooking.
She hauled heavy buckets from the well, but after several trips
the jar was no more full than before. "Oh!" she cried when she
found a hole at the bottom. "Doki will be angry if my work is
not done."

"Rrrribbit. I will help you, Kongi," said a plump toad who
leaped into the jar and plugged up the hole with his ample body.

How lucky I am to have such good friends, thought Kongi, glad
that she could now join the celebration.

Kongi and Potgi soon grew to be young women. One day some
exciting news came from the palace. The prince was seeking
a bride, and a great party would be held in his honor. All of the
eligible young ladies were invited!

The people were jubilant. Every young woman counted the
days, and Kongi and Potgi were no exceptions. Under her mother's
watchful eye Potgi tried on new clothes and arranged her hair,
until everything seemed just right.

When the big day came, Kongi too hoped to go to the palace.
But Doki had other ideas. She told Kongi to take the bundles of
grain from the bin, let the grain dry, and remove each kernel of
rice from its hard outer shell. "When the rice jar is full, you may
come to the palace," she said, closing the door behind her.

How could her stepmother be so cruel? As Kongi spread the
grain out to dry, she felt sad and alone.

Suddenly a hundred little sparrows encircled her, singing,
"Chirp, chirp. Don't cry, Kongi. We will help you. Then off to the
palace you'll go!" Kongi watched as they used their beaks to peck
out the grain, and flapped their wings to carry the hulls away in
the breeze. Before long the job was done.

Kongi sat on the ground and gazed up at the sky. Despondent, she thought of her mother and began to cry. I could never go to the palace in these rags anyway, she thought hopelessly.

Just then a brilliant rainbow filled the sky, and radiant angels drifted down from the clouds. Kongi was sure that she must be dreaming. They dressed her in the finest silks and the loveliest shoes, embroidered with the tiniest of stitches. Suddenly four men carrying a sedan chair appeared in the yard, ready to take her to the party.

As Kongi arrived at the palace, the sounds of music and laughter filled the air. But when she entered the room, all eyes turned to her, so great was her beauty. Even the prince was captivated by her presence. "What is your name? What village do you come from?" he asked.

Flustered by the prince's attentions, Kongi's face turned a deep crimson and her heart began to pound, until she could sit still no longer.

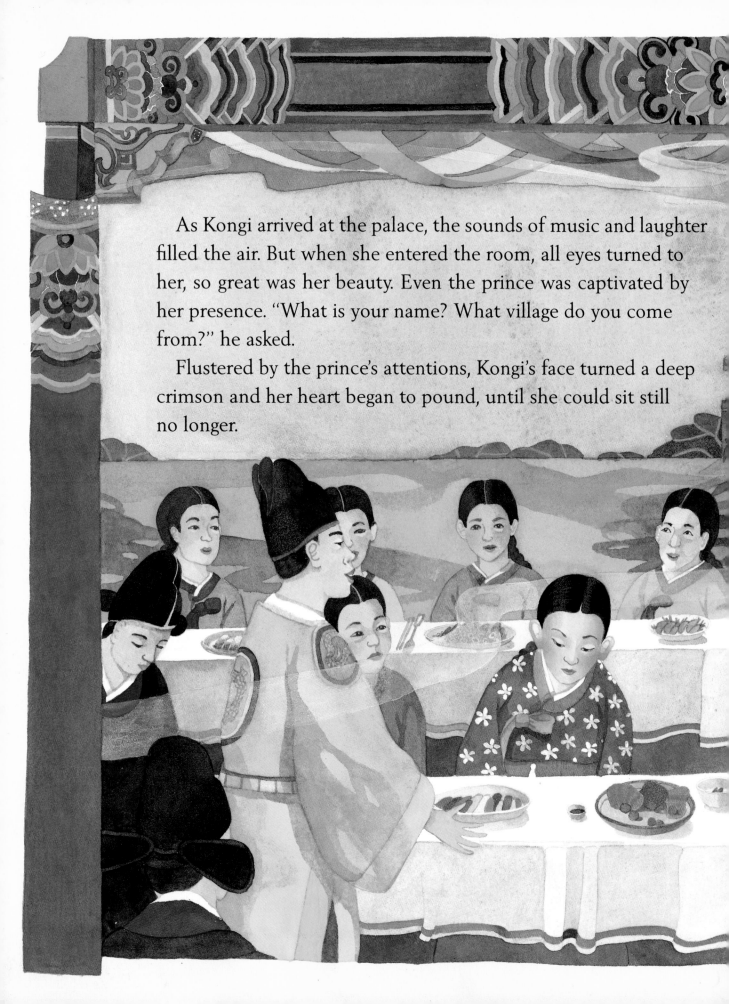

She gathered up her skirt and ran from the room without looking back.

"Miss, wait! Where are you going?" called the prince, trying to make his way through the crowd. But it was no use. Kongi was gone.

The prince turned sadly back to the ball, when suddenly something caught his eye. A jewellike slipper, finer than any he had seen, lay before him. He knew at once that it must belong to the mysterious young woman.

Doki and Potgi returned home late that night, and spoke of nothing but the strange girl who had so enchanted the prince. "What a shame that you couldn't make it, Kongi," said her stepmother.

Kongi smiled, but said nothing.

Within days the search began for the owner of the slipper. Palace horsemen rode from town to town, and finally came to Kongi's village.

Young women of every shape and size clamored to try on the elegant shoe. As each presented her foot, it appeared that the slipper was just her size. But that wasn't the case.

"That shoe is surely enchanted," they cried. "It seems to change its size at whim!"

But Doki listened to not a word. "That shoe belongs to my Potgi," she said, stuffing her daughter's foot into the tiny shoe, until it almost burst at the seams.

"Next!" cried the groom.

Doki tried to push Kongi away. "You are wasting your time," she protested, to no avail.

Kongi's foot slid easily into the slipper, which couldn't have fit her more perfectly. Potgi and her mother were dumbstruck as Kongi produced the matching shoe.

When Kongi arrived at the palace, the prince was overjoyed to have found his princess. The villagers celebrated the news of their wedding.

At the wedding reception Doki and Potgi could barely look at the bride, for they were ashamed of the way they had treated her. But Kongi welcomed them warmly and forgave their unkindness. Her father could not have been more proud.

Soon the prince was crowned king and Kongi queen. The two were loved and respected throughout the land and ruled their kingdom wisely. Over the years Kongi had learned to be patient, humble, and kind—qualities that helped her to serve her people well. Even Doki and Potgi praised her, and spent the rest of their days helping others and doing good deeds.